Favorite Fairy Tales
Retold by
Virginia Haviland

Favorite Fairy Tales

TOLD IN ITALY

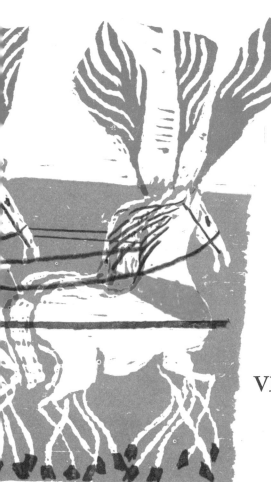

Favorite Fairy Tales

TOLD
IN
ITALY

Retold by
VIRGINIA HAVILAND

Illustrated by
EVALINE NESS

Boston **LITTLE, BROWN AND COMPANY** *Toronto*

LIBRARY OF CONGRESS CATALOG CARD NO. 65–13715

FIRST EDITION

Third Printing

These stories have been retold from the following sources:

CENERENTOLA and THE STONE IN THE COCK'S HEAD are retold from
Giambattista Basile's STORIES FROM THE PENTAMERONE, selected
and edited by E. F. Strange (London, Macmillan, 1911), which
follow the translation by John Edward Taylor, 1847. CENERENTOLA
is a Neapolitan tale.

THE STORY OF BENSURDATU is retold from Andrew Lang's GREY FAIRY
BOOK (New York, Longmans, Green and Company, 1900) where
it is translated from L. Gonzenbach's SICILIANISCHE MARCHEN
(Leipzig, 1870).

BASTIANELO and THE THREE GOSLINGS are retold from Thomas F.
Crane's ITALIAN POPULAR TALES (Boston, Houghton Mifflin Com-
pany, 1885). BASTIANELO is a Venetian tale collected by Dom
Giuseppe Bernoni in his FIABE POPULARI VENEZIANI, 1873.

THE GOLDEN LION is retold from Andrew Lang's PINK FAIRY BOOK
(New York, Longmans, Green and Company, 1897), also from
the SICILIANISCHE MARCHEN.

Published simultaneously in Canada
by Little, Brown & Company (Canada) Limited

PRINTED IN THE UNITED STATES OF AMERICA

Contents

Cenerentola

ONCE THERE LIVED a Prince whose wife died and left him with an only daughter named Zezolla. So dear to him was the girl that he saw with no other eyes than hers. He employed a governess for her, who loved her and taught her how to knit and to make lace. But Zezolla was very lonely. Many a time she said to her governess, "Oh, I do wish you were my mother. You show me such kindness and love."

She repeated this so often that, at last, the governess said to her, "Indeed, if you will do as I advise, I shall become your mother, and you shall be as dear to me as the apple of my eye."

The governess was going to say more, but Zezolla said, "Enough. Only show me the way."

"Well, then," answered the governess, "open your ears and listen. When your father is caressing you, do you entreat him to marry me and make me Princess. Then you shall be the mistress of my life!"

After Zezolla heard this, each hour seemed a thousand years long until she was able to do as her governess advised. When the mourning for her mother was ended, Zezolla began to beg her father to marry her governess. At first the Prince took it only lightly, but Zezolla went on until he gave way. He married the governess, then, and gave a great feast at the wedding.

Now, while the young people were dancing, and Zezolla was standing at the window, a dove flew over and perched on the wall. It said to her, "Whenever you need anything, send your request to the Dove of the Fairies in the Island of Sardinia, and instantly you will have what you desire."

For five or six days, the new stepmother nearly smothered Zezolla with affection. She gave her choice morsels to eat and clothed her in rich dresses. But before long, she brought forward six daughters of her own, though she had never told anyone that she was a widow with all these girls. She began to praise them and to talk about them to the Prince in such a way that at last the step-daughters had won all his favor. Thoughts of Zezolla, his own child, went right out of his heart. In short, it began to go so ill with the poor girl that she was sent from the royal chamber down to the kitchen, and even her name was changed. Instead of Zezolla, she was called Cenerentola, which in another language means Cinderella.

One day it happened that the Prince had to go to Sardinia on affairs of state. Calling to him the six stepdaughters, he asked them, one by one, what they would like him to bring them on his return. One wished for beautiful dresses, another to have some head ornaments, another rouge for the face, another toys and trinkets — one wished for this and another for that. At last the Prince turned to his own daughter and asked, as if in mockery, "And what would you have, child?"

"Nothing, Father," Cenerentola replied, "but commend me to the Dove of the Fairies, and bid her send me something. And if you forget my request, may you be unable to stir backwards or forwards. Remember what I tell you, for it will fare with you accordingly."

The Prince then went on his way and took care of his business in Sardinia. He procured all the things his stepdaughters had asked for, but he quite forgot Cenerentola. When he boarded his ship to return, the ship could not get out of the harbor. It stuck there fast, as if held by a sea creature. The captain of the ship, who was tired out and almost in despair, laid himself down to sleep. In his dream he saw a fairy, who asked him, "Know you not the reason why you cannot sail the ship out of port? It is because the Prince who is on board has broken his promise to his daughter."

The captain awoke and told his dream to the Prince, who in shame and confusion went at once to the Grotto of the Fairies. He commended his daughter to them and asked them to send her something. At once there stepped forth from the grotto a beautiful maiden, who told him that she thanked his daughter for her kind remembrances. She bade him tell her to be merry and of good heart. She gave him a date tree, a golden hoe with which to hoe it, a small golden bucket with which to water it, and a silken napkin with which to wipe its leaves.

The Prince, marveling at all this, took leave of the fairy. He was now able to sail away and return to his own country. After he had presented his stepdaughters with all the things they had asked for, he gave his own daughter her gifts from the fairy. Cenerentola, overjoyed, planted the date tree in a pretty pot; she hoed the earth around it, watered it, and wiped its leaves morning and evening with the silken napkin.

In a few days the tree had grown as tall as a woman. And out of it stepped a fairy, who asked Cenerentola, "What is your wish?"

Cenerentola answered that she wished sometimes to leave the house without her sisters' knowing it.

The fairy quickly answered, "Whenever you desire this, come to the flower pot and say:

> *My little date tree, my golden tree,*
> *With a golden hoe I have hoed thee,*
> *With a golden can I have watered thee,*
> *With a silken cloth I have wiped thee dry,*
> *Now strip thee and dress me speedily.*

And when you wish to remove your new garments, change the last words and say, '*Strip me and dress thee.*'"

Soon there came the eve of a great feast. The stepsisters appeared bedecked elegantly, in ribbons and flowers, slippers and bells. It made Cenerentola run to the flower pot, to repeat the words the fairy had given her. At once she found herself arrayed like a queen, far more splendid than her stepsisters. She was seated upon a fine horse, and attended by twelve smart pages, all in bright raiment.

Off Cenerentola rode to the ball, where she

made the sisters envious of an unknown beauty. The young King himself attended the ball, and as soon as he saw Cenerentola, he stood magic-bound with enchantment. He kept his eyes on her all evening, and when she left he ordered a servant to find out who this beautiful maiden was, and where she lived.

The servant followed Cenerentola, but when she noticed this she threw on the ground a handful of coins which she had got from the date tree. The servant stopped, lighted his lantern, and became so busy picking up all the coins that he quite forgot to follow her. Cenerentola was able to get home safely and change her clothes before the wicked sisters arrived.

The sisters, trying to make her envious, told her of all the fine things they had seen, but were quite unable to vex her.

The King was angry with his servant and warned him next time not to lose her.

Before long another ball was announced. Again

the sisters went off to it, all bedecked in their finery, not at all concerned to leave poor Cenerentola at home on the kitchen hearth.

But Cenerentola, as soon as they disappeared, ran to the date tree and repeated the chant. Instantly there appeared a number of handmaidens: one with a looking glass, another with sweet-smelling rose water, others with curling irons and combs, and pins, and rich apparel to dress her in. They groomed her so that she shone as gloriously as the sun, and they put her in a coach drawn by six white horses, attended by footmen and pages in handsome livery.

No sooner did Cenerentola appear in the ballroom than the sisters were struck with amazement. And the King was quite overcome with love. His eyes never left her all evening.

When Cenerentola departed, the servant was again instructed to follow her. This time she was prepared with a handful of pearls. Seeing that these were not things to lose, the servant dropped

behind to pick them up. And again she managed to slip away and remove her fine dress before her stepsisters saw her in it.

Meanwhile the servant had returned slowly to the King, who cried out angrily when he saw him without the beautiful girl. "By the souls of my ancestors, if you do not find out who she is, you shall have such a thrashing as was never heard of before, and as many kicks as you have hairs in your beard!"

When the next ball was held, and the sisters were safely out of the house, Cenerentola went again to the date tree, and once more repeated the chant. In an instant she found herself splendidly arrayed and seated in a coach of gold, with ever so many servants around her. She looked like a queen and made the sisters beside themselves with envy.

This time, when Cenerentola left the ballroom after the dancing, the King's servant kept close to the coach. She saw him running by the coach and cried to the coachman to drive on quickly. The

coach set off at such a rattling pace that Cenerentola lost one of her beautiful slippers. The servant, being unable to keep up with the coach now,
picked up the slipper and, carrying it to the King,
told him all that had happened.

The King, turning the slipper around in his
hand, said, "You, indeed, are so beautiful it is no
wonder that you belong to her. You who impris-
oned her white foot are now binding my unhappy
heart!"

The King then made a proclamation that all
the women in the country should come to a ban-
quet. For it, the most splendid provision was
made — of pastas and pastries, of macaroni and
sweetmeats — enough to feed an entire army.
And when all the women were assembled, noble
and lowly, rich and poor, beautiful and ugly, the
King tried the slipper on each one. Thus he should
see whom it fitted to a hair, and thus be able to
discover the maiden he sought. But not one foot
could fit the slipper.

When the King asked whether indeed every woman in the country was there, the Prince had to confess that he had one daughter at home. "But," said he, "Cenerentola sits always on the hearth, such a dirty, graceless girl that she is unworthy to come to your table."

But the King answered, "Let her be the very first, for so I order it."

All the guests departed, but the next day they assembled again, and with the ugly sisters came Cenerentola.

When the King saw Cenerentola, he began to wonder. But he said nothing.

After the feast came the trial of the slipper. This, as soon as ever it came near Cenerentola's foot, darted onto it as if of its own accord. The King ran to her, took her in his arms, and seated her under his royal canopy with a crown upon her head. And thereupon everyone bowed to her as their Queen.

The Story of Bensurdatu

THERE WERE ONCE a King and Queen who had three wonderfully beautiful daughters. Their one thought, from morning till night, was how to make the Princesses happy.

One day the Princesses said to the King, "Dear Father, we want so much to have a picnic in the country."

"Very well, dear children, let us have a picnic, by all means," and he gave orders that everything should be made ready.

When luncheon was prepared it was put into a cart. The royal family stepped into a carriage and drove away into the country. After riding a few miles, they reached a house and garden belonging to the King. Close by was their favorite place for picnicking. Since the drive had made them hungry, they ate directly and with such a hearty appetite that almost all the food disappeared.

When they had eaten their fill, the Princesses said to their parents, "Now we should like to play about the garden a little, but when you want to go home, just call to us."

Off they ran, laughing, down a green glade. But no sooner had they stepped over a fence than a dark cloud came down and covered them, so that they could not see where they were going.

Meanwhile the King and Queen sat lazily among the flowers. An hour and more slipped away. The sun was dropping toward the horizon, and they knew it was time to go home. They called to their daughters. They called again, and again, but they had no answer.

Frightened by this silence, they searched every corner of the garden, the house, and the neighboring wood, but no trace of the girls was to be found.

The earth seemed to have swallowed them up. The poor parents were in despair.

The Queen wept all the way home, and for many days after. And the King issued a proclamation that whosoever would bring back his lost daughters should have one of them as wife and should, after the King's death, reign in his stead.

Now two young knights were at that time living at the court, and when they heard the King's declaration they said, one to the other, "Let us go in search of the Princesses. Perhaps we shall be the lucky persons."

And they set out, each mounted on a strong horse, taking with them a change of raiment and some money.

But though they inquired at every village they rode through, they could hear nothing of the Princesses. After a time, their money was all spent, and they were forced to sell their horses or give up the search. But the money they received lasted only a little while longer, and nothing then but their clothes lay between them and starvation.

They sold the spare garments they had bound on their saddles, and went to an inn to beg for some food, for they were close to starving. When, however, they had to pay for what they had eaten and drunk, they said to the innkeeper:

"We have no money, and naught but the clothes we stand up in. Take these and give us instead some old rags, and let us stay here and serve you."

The innkeeper was content with this bargain, so the knights stayed and became his servants.

All this time the King and Queen remained in their palace, longing for their children's return, but not a word was heard either of the Princesses or of the young men who had gone to seek them.

Now there was living in the palace a faithful servant of the King's called Bensurdatu, who had served him for many years. When Bensurdatu saw how deeply the King grieved, he went to him and said, "Your Majesty, let me go and seek your daughters."

"No, no, Bensurdatu," replied the King. "Three daughters have I lost, and two knights. Shall I lose you also?"

But Bensurdatu said again, "Let me now go, Your Majesty. Trust me, and I will bring you back your daughters."

The King gave way and Bensurdatu set forth. He rode on till he came to the inn, where he dismounted and asked for food. It was brought by the two knights, whom he knew at once in spite of the old rags they wore. Much astonished, he asked them how they came to be here, in this state.

When the knights told him of their adventures, he sent for the innkeeper and said, "Give them back their garments and I will pay everything they owe you."

The innkeeper did as he was bade. When the two knights were dressed in their proper clothes, they declared they would join Bensurdatu and with him seek the King's daughters.

The three companions rode on for many miles,

and at length came to a wild place, without sign
of a human being. Fearing to be lost in this deso-
late spot, in the growing dark, they pushed on till
at last they saw a light in the window of a small
hut.

"Who comes here?" asked a voice, as they
knocked at the door.

"Oh, have pity on us, and give us a night's
shelter," replied Bensurdatu. "We are three tired
travelers who have lost our way."

The door was opened by a very old woman, who
stood back and beckoned them to enter. "Whence
do you come, and whither do you go?" asked she.

"Ah, good woman, we have a heavy task before

us," answered Bensurdatu. "We are bound to carry the King's daughters back to the palace!"

"Oh, unhappy creatures," cried she, "you know not what you are doing! The King's daughters were covered by a thick cloud, and no one knows where they may now be."

"Oh, tell us, if you know, my good woman," entreated Bensurdatu, "for with them lies all our happiness."

"Even if I were to tell you," answered she, "you could not rescue them. To do that you would have to go to the very bottom of a deep river. Though certainly you would find the King's daughters there, you would see the two eldest guarded by two giants and the youngest watched by a serpent with seven heads."

The two knights, who stood by listening, were filled with terror at her words. They wished to return immediately, but Bensurdatu stood firm, and said, "Now we have come so far we must carry through. Tell us where the river is, good woman, so that we may get there as soon as possible."

The old woman directed them and gave them cheese, wine and bread so they should not set forth starving. When they had eaten and drunk, they laid themselves down to sleep.

The sun had only just risen above the hills next morning when they all awoke. Taking leave of the wise woman who had helped them, they then rode on till at length they came to the river she had described.

"I am the eldest," said one of the knights, "and it is my right to go down first."

The others fastened a cord around him, gave him a little bell, and let him down into the water. But scarcely had the river closed above his head when such dreadful rushing sounds and peals of thunder came crashing round about him that he lost all his courage. He rang his bell, hoping it might be heard amidst all this clamor. Great was his relief when the rope began slowly to pull him upward.

The other knight plunged in next, but he fared no better than the first, and was soon pulled out on dry ground again.

"Well, you are a brave pair!" said Bensurdatu, as he tied the rope round his own waist. "Let us see what will happen to me." Down he went, and when he heard the thunder and clamor round about him he said to himself, "Oh, make as much noise as you like, it won't hurt me!"

When his feet touched the bottom, he found himself in a large, brilliantly lighted hall. In the middle sat the eldest Princess, and in front of her lay a huge giant, fast asleep. Directly she saw Bensurdatu she nodded to him and asked with her eyes how he had come there.

For answer he drew his sword, and was about to cut off the giant's head when she stopped him quickly and made signs to him to hide, as the giant was just beginning to wake.

"I smell the flesh of a man!" murmured he, stretching his great arms.

"How in the world could any man get down here?" asked the Princess. "You had better go to sleep again."

So he turned over and went to sleep. The Princess signaled to Bensurdatu, who drew his sword and cut off the giant's head with such a blow that it flew into the corner. The Princess's heart leaped within her, and she placed a golden crown on the head of Bensurdatu and called him her deliverer.

"Now show me where your sisters are," he said, "that I may free them also."

The Princess opened a door and led him into another hall, where sat her next sister, also guarded by a giant who was fast asleep. When this Princess saw them, she made a sign to them to hide, for the giant was showing signs of waking.

"I smell man's flesh!" murmured he, sleepily.

"Now, how could any man get down here?" asked she. "Go to sleep again."

And as soon as the giant closed his eyes, Bensurdatu stole out from his corner and struck such a blow with his sword that the giant's head flew far, far away. The Princess could not find words to thank Bensurdatu for what he had done, and she too gave him a golden crown.

"Now show me where your youngest sister is," said he, "that I may free her also."

"Ah, that we fear you will never be able to do," sighed they, "for she is in the power of a serpent with seven heads."

"Take me to him," replied Bensurdatu. "It will be a splendid fight."

The Princess opened a door. Bensurdatu passed through and found himself in a hall even larger than the other two. And there stood the youngest sister, chained fast to the wall. Before her stretched a serpent with seven heads, horrible to see.

As Bensurdatu came forward, the serpent twisted all its seven heads in his direction and made a quick dart to snatch him within its grasp. But Bensurdatu drew his sword and laid it about him till the seven heads were rolling on the floor. Flinging down his sword, Bensurdatu rushed to the Princess and broke her chains, while she wept for joy and embraced him. She took her gold crown off her head and placed it in his hand.

"Now we must go back to the upper world," said Bensurdatu, and led her to the bottom of the river. The other Princesses sat waiting there. He tied his rope around the eldest and rang his bell. The knights above heard and drew her up gently. They then unfastened the rope and threw it back into the river. In a few moments the second Princess stood beside her sister.

Now there were left only Bensurdatu and the youngest Princess. "Dear Bensurdatu," said she, "do me a kindness and let them draw you up before me. I fear treachery from the knights."

"No, no," replied Bensurdatu. "I certainly will not leave you down here. There is nothing to fear from my comrades."

"If it is your wish, I will go up. But first I swear that if you do not follow, to marry me, I shall stay single for the rest of my life."

Bensurdatu bound the rope around the lovely youngest Princess and the knights drew her up.

Now Bensurdatu's courage and success so filled

the hearts of the two knights with envy that they turned away, instead of lowering the rope again into the river, and they left him to perish. More than that, they threatened the Princesses and forced them to promise to tell their parents that it was the two knights who had set them free. "And if they ask you about Bensurdatu, you must say you have never seen him," they added. The Princesses, fearing for their lives, promised everything, and they rode back to court together.

The King and Queen were beside themselves with joy when they saw their dear children once more. When the knights had told their story and described the dangers they had run, the King declared that they had gained their reward and the two eldest Princesses should become their wives.

In the meantime, poor Bensurdatu was waiting patiently. But after a long time, when the rope did not come back, he knew that he had been wrong and that his comrades had betrayed him.

"Ah, now I shall never reach the world again,"

murmured he. But being a brave man and knowing that bemoaning his fate would profit him nothing, he rose and began to search through the three halls. There, perhaps, he might find something to help him. In the last one stood a dish of food, which reminded him that he was hungry, so he sat down and ate and drank.

Months had passed away when one morning, as he was walking through the halls, he noticed hanging on the wall a purse, which had not been there before. He took it down to examine it, and nearly let it fall when a voice came from it, saying, "What commands have you, my lord?"

"Oh, take me out of this horrible place and up into the world again!" In a moment he was standing by the river bank, with the purse tightly grasped in his hand.

"Now let me have the most beautiful ship that ever was built, all manned and ready for the sea."

And there was the ship, with a flag floating from its mast on which were the words *King with the three crowns*. At once Bensurdatu climbed on board and sailed away to the city where the three Princesses dwelt. When he reached the harbor he blew trumpets and beat drums, so that everyone ran to their doors and windows.

The King heard, too, and saw the beautiful vessel. To himself he said, "That must indeed be a mighty monarch, for he has three crowns while I have only one." He hastened forth to greet the stranger, and invited him into his castle. "This man," thought he, "will be a fine husband for my youngest daughter." It was true that the youngest Princess had turned a deaf ear to all her wooers.

Such a long time had passed since Bensurdatu had left the palace, the King never guessed for a moment that this splendidly clad stranger was the man he had mourned as dead.

"Noble lord," said he, "let us feast and make merry together, and then, if it seem good to you, do me the honor to take my youngest daughter as your wife."

Bensurdatu was delighted to join them in a lavish feast, where there was great rejoicing. But only the youngest daughter was sad, for her thoughts were with Bensurdatu. After they arose from the table, the King said to her, "Dear child, this mighty lord does you the honor to ask your hand in marriage."

"Oh, Father," answered she, "spare me, I pray you, for I desire to remain single."

Then Bensurdatu turned to her, and said, "And if I were Bensurdatu, would you give the same answer to me?"

As she stood silently gazing at him, he added, "Yes, I am Bensurdatu, and this is my story."

The King and Queen felt their hearts stir within them at his tale of adventures. When he had ended, the King stretched out his hand and said, "Dear Bensurdatu, my youngest daughter shall indeed be your wife, and when I die my crown shall be yours. As for the men who have betrayed you, they shall leave the country and you shall see them no more."

A wedding feast was now ordered, and the rejoicing over the marriage of Bensurdatu and the beautiful youngest Princess lasted for three days.

The Stone in the Cock's Head

THERE WAS ONCE in the city of Dark Grotto a certain man named Minecco, who had such bad luck that finally he owned only a short-legged cock which he had reared upon bread crumbs.

One morning Minecco was so hungry that he decided to sell the cock. Taking it to market, he met two thievish magicians with whom he made a bargain — to sell the cock for half a crown. The thieves told him to take the cock to their house and they would count out the money for him.

They went on their way, but Minecco followed them and overheard them say, one to the other, "Who would have told us that we would meet with such good luck? This cock will make our fortune with that magic stone in his head. We shall have it set in a ring and then we shall have everything we ask for."

When Minecco, who was no fool, heard this, he turned and ran home with the cock. He himself removed the stone from the cock's head and had it set in a brass ring. With it on his finger, he made a wish: "I desire to become again a youth eighteen years old."

Hardly had the words left his mouth when his limbs began to feel more firm. His silver hairs turned to gold and his mouth regained its lost teeth. He had become a most handsome youth.

Now, he added, "I should like to live in a splendid palace and to marry a King's daughter." Lo, there appeared at once a palace of incredible magnificence, with endless richly furnished rooms. Decorated columns, beautiful pictures, and glittering floors dazzled the eyes, and servants swarmed like ants. Outside stood horses and carriages beyond counting. In short, such a display of riches burst into view that the King was impressed and willingly gave Minecco his daughter Natalizia for his bride.

Meanwhile, however, the magicians discovered Minecco's fabulous wealth and began plotting to rob him of his good fortune. They devised a pretty little doll which could play and dance when wound up. Then, dressing like merchants, they took it to Minecco's daughter, Pentella, under pretext of selling it to her. When Pentella saw the amusing toy, she asked them what price they were asking for it. But they replied that it could not be bought for money; she might have it and welcome — if she would only do them a favor. She must let them examine the ring which her father possessed, in order that they might make another like it. When she managed this, they would give her the doll.

Pentella had never heard the proverb, "Think well before you buy anything cheap," so she accepted this offer at once. Bidding them return the next morning, she promised to ask her father to lend her the ring.

The magicians went away, and on her father's

return Pentella coaxed him until at last she persuaded him to give her the ring.

Early the next day, the magicians returned. As soon as they had the ring in their hands they vanished, leaving poor Pentella shaking with fear.

When the magicians came to a wood, they asked the ring to break the spell by which old Minecco had become young and handsome. Instantly Minecco, who just at that moment had entered the presence of the King, was seen to grow aged; his hair became white and his forehead lined with wrinkles. His eyes sank into his face and his mouth lost its teeth again, while his legs trembled. Instead of fine clothing he wore tattered rags.

The King, seeing a miserable beggar beside him, ordered him away. Thereupon Minecco, thus fallen from his good luck, went weeping to his daughter and asked for the ring, in order to set matters right again.

When he heard of the trick played by the false merchants, he raged at his foolish daughter, who for the sake of a silly doll had turned him into a wretched scarecrow. He vowed to wander about the world until he should find those merchants.

Minecco threw an old cloak about his shoulders, fastened on his sandals, and hung a wallet of bread and cheese on his back. He took a staff in his hand and set out, leaving his daughter overcome with remorse.

Full of despair he walked, until he arrived at the kingdom of Deep Hole, which is inhabited by mice. Here they took him for a great spy of the cats and instantly led him before their King. The King of the mice asked him who he was, whence he came, and what he was about that he came to their country. Minecco offered him a cheese paring, in tribute, then related all his misfortunes, saying finally that he was resolved to continue his travel until he should find those thievish magicians.

The King of the mice felt pity stirring in his heart, and to comfort the poor man he summoned the oldest mice to a council. He asked their opinions on Minecco's misfortunes. Also, he commanded them to use all their cleverness to locate those false merchants. Now, among them were two good mice who were used to the ways of the world. They had lived for six years at a tavern nearby. To Minecco they offered encouragement. "Be of good heart! Matters will turn out better than you imagine. You must know that one day, when we were at the inn where famous men of the world stop and make merry, there came two persons from Hook Castle. After they had eaten and drunk their fill, they fell to talking of a trick they had played on a certain old man of Dark Grotto. They told how they had cheated him out of a stone of great value, set in a ring which one of them was wearing and said he would never take from his finger, lest he lose it as the old man's daughter had done."

When Minecco heard this, he told the two mice that if they would go with him to the country of

these rogues and recover the ring, he would reward them with good cheese and bacon. The two mice agreed, and taking leave of their King, they set out with Minecco.

After journeying many miles over sea and mountains, the three arrived at Hook Castle. The mice told Minecco to rest under some trees by the river while they went to seek out the rogues.

At night, when the magicians had gone to bed and were fast asleep, one of the mice began to nibble the finger wearing the ring. Feeling the sharp teeth, as if the ring made the finger smart, the magician took the ring off and laid it on the table beside his bed. And now the other mouse, waiting, popped the ring into his mouth and in four skips was off to find Minecco.

With the ring on his finger again, Minecco immediately turned the two thieves into donkeys. Over one he threw his mantle, to ride him; on the other he loaded cheese and bacon — and they set off toward Deep Hole.

In the kingdom of the mice, Minecco gave presents all around and thanked them all for restoring his good fortune. He prayed Heaven that no mousetrap would ever lay hold of them and no cat ever harm them.

Leaving their friendly country, Minecco returned to Dark Grotto, appearing even more handsome than before. The King and his daughter, recognizing him, received him with great affection. Minecco lived henceforth most happily with his wife, and never again did he take the ring from his finger.

Bastianelo

ONCE UPON A TIME there were a husband and wife who had a son. When the son grew up, he said one day to his mother, "Do you know, Mother, I would like to marry!"

"Very well, marry! Whom do you want to take for a bride?"

The son answered, "I want the gardener's daughter."

"She is a good girl; I am willing," said his mother.

He went and asked for the girl and her parents gave her to him, so they were married. All was merry but in the midst of the wedding dinner the wine gave out. When the young husband cried, "There is no more wine!" the bride, to show that she was a good housekeeper, at once went to get some.

She carried the bottles to the cellar, turned the cock on the wine keg, and, waiting for the bottles to fill, began to think, "Suppose I should have a son, and we should call him Bastianelo, and he should die. Oh, how I should grieve! Oh, how I should grieve!" Thereupon she began to weep and wail, and the wine ran all over the cellar floor.

When the others saw that the bride did not return, her mother said, "I will go and see what the matter is." So she went into the cellar, and saw the bride, with a bottle in her hand, weeping while the wine ran over the cellar. "What is it that makes you weep?"

"Ah! Mother, I was thinking that if I had a son and should name him Bastianelo, and he should die, oh, how I should grieve! Oh, how I should grieve!"

At this the mother, too, began to weep, and weep, and weep. And the wine ran all over the cellar.

When the people still at the table saw that no

one was bringing the wine, the groom's father said, "I will go and see what is the matter. Certainly something has happened to the bride." He found the cellar full of wine, and the mother and bride weeping.

"What is the matter?" he asked. "Has anything wrong happened?"

"No," answered the bride, "but I was thinking that if I had a son and should call him Bastianelo, and he should die, oh, how I should grieve. Oh, how I should grieve!"

At this the father, too, began to weep. All three wept, and the wine ran all over the cellar.

When the groom saw that neither the bride nor the mother nor father came back, he decided, "Now I will go and see what the matter is." He went into the cellar and saw all the wine running over the cellar floor.

He hastened to stop the flow of wine, and then asked, "What is the matter that you are all weeping, and have let the wine run all over the cellar?"

The bride admitted, "I was thinking that if I had a son and called him Bastianelo, and he should die, oh, how I should grieve! Oh, how I should grieve!"

The groom was astonished. "You stupid fools! Are you weeping at this and letting all the wine run into the cellar? Have you nothing else to think of? It shall never be said that I married such a one as you! I shall travel forth into the world, and until I find three fools greater than you I shall not return here."

So the young man had a bread cake made for him, took a bottle of wine, a sausage, a change of clothing, and made up a bundle, which he tied on a stick and carried over his shoulder.

Day after day he journeyed and journeyed, but found no fools. At last, worn out, he was undecided whether to go on or to turn back. But then he said, "Oh, it is better to try a little longer."

So on he went, and shortly saw a man in his shirtsleeves at a well, all wet with perspiration and water. "What are you doing, sir, that you are so covered with water and in such a sweat?"

"Oh, let me alone!" the man answered. "I have been here a long time drawing water to fill this pail and I cannot fill it."

"What are you drawing the water in?" he asked the man.

"In this sieve."

"What are you thinking of, trying to draw water in a sieve? Just wait!" The young man went to a house nearby and borrowed a bucket. With this he returned to the well and filled the pail.

"Thank you, good man. God knows how long I should have had to remain here!"

"Here is one," said the young man, "who is a greater fool than my wife."

He continued his journey, and after a time saw at a distance a man in his shirt who was jumping from a tree. He drew near and saw a woman under the same tree holding a pair of breeches. When he asked them what they were doing, they said they

had been there a long time. The man was trying on the breeches and did not know how to get into them. "I have jumped and jumped," said the man, "until I am tired out, and I still cannot imagine how to get into those breeches."

"Well," said the traveler, "you might stay here forever. You would never get into them this way. Come down, now, and lean against the tree."

He took the man's legs then and put them into the breeches. After he had done this, he asked, "Is that right?"

"Very good, bless you," said the man. "If it had not been for you, God knows how long I should have had to continue jumping."

Now the traveler said to himself, "I have seen two fools greater than my wife." And he went on his way.

As he approached a city he heard a great noise. When he drew near he asked what it was all about, and learned that there was a wedding. It was the custom in that city for brides to enter the city

gate on horseback. This time there was going on a great discussion between the groom and the owner of the horse, for the bride was tall and the horse was high. They could not get through the gate; either they must cut off the bride's head or chop off the horse's legs. The groom naturally did not wish his bride's head cut off, and the owner of the horse refused to have his horse lose his legs. Hence the uproar.

The traveler said, "Wait." He turned to the bride and slapped the top of her head so that she

lowered it. At the same time he kicked the horse. They passed through the gate into the city.

In return for this help, the groom and the owner of the horse asked the young man what present they could give him. He answered that he did not wish for anything, and to himself counted, "Two and one make three! That is enough! Now I will go home."

This he did, and said to his wife, "Here I am, my wife; I have seen three greater fools than you. Let us remain in peace and think of nothing else."

Now they went on with the wedding celebration, and always after that they lived in peace.

After a time the wife bore a son whom they named Bastianelo — but Bastianelo did not die. He still lives with his father and mother.

The Three Goslings

ONCE UPON A TIME there were three goslings who were much afraid of a great big wolf. They knew that if he found them, he would eat them alive. One day the largest gosling said to the other two, "Do you know what I think? I think we had better build a little house, so that the wolf shall not eat us. Let us go at once and look for something with which to build the house."

The other two goslings answered, "Yes, yes, yes . . . good! Let us go!"

So they went together and found a man who had a load of straw. "Good man," they cried, "do us the kindness to give us a little of your straw to make a house of, so that the wolf shall not eat us."

The man said, "Take it, take it!" and he gave them as much as they needed.

The goslings cried out their thanks and waddled off with the straw to a meadow. There they built a fine little house, with a door, and balconies, and kitchen — with everything one could want.

When the house was finished, the largest gosling said, "Now I want to see whether one will be comfortable in this house." So she went in and then called out, "Oh, how comfortable it is in this house! Just wait!" With that she locked the door with a padlock, went out on the balcony, and called down to the other two goslings, "I am very comfortable here alone. Go away! I want nothing to do with you!"

The two poor little goslings began to weep and beg their sister to open the door and let them in. If she did not, they cried, the wolf would eat them. But the largest gosling would not listen to them.

The two goslings went away and found a man who had a load of hay. "Good man," they cried, "do us the kindness to give us a little of that hay

to make a house of, so that the wolf shall not eat us!"

"Yes, yes, yes, take some, take some!" And the man gave them as much as they needed.

The two goslings, well pleased, thanked the man and carried the hay to a meadow. Here they built a little house even prettier than the other.

The middle-sized gosling now said to the smallest one, "Listen. I am going now to see whether one will be comfortable in this house. But I shall not act like our sister, you know!" She entered the house and thought to herself, "Oh, how comfortable it is here! I don't want my sister! I am very comfortable here alone." She fastened the door with a lock and went out on the balcony and said to her sister, "Oh, how comfortable it is in this house! I don't want you here! Go away, go away."

The poor smallest gosling began to weep and beg her sister to open the door to her, for she was alone and did not know where to go. If the wolf found her he would eat her, she said. But it did no good. Her sister shut the balcony door and stayed in the house.

The smallest gosling, full of fear, went away and found a man who had a load of iron and stones. "Good man," she cried, "do me the kindness to give me a few of those stones and a little of that iron so that I may build a house and the wolf will not eat me!"

The man pitied the little gosling so much that he answered, "Yes, yes, good gosling. And I will build your house for you."

Off they went together to a meadow, where the man built a very good house, with a garden and everything necessary. And it was a very strong house, too, for it was lined with iron, and the balcony and door were made of iron, also. The gosling, well pleased, thanked the man and went into her house and remained there.

The wolf looked everywhere for the goslings, but could not find them. After a time he learned that they had built three different houses. "Good,

good!" he thought. "Wait until I find you!"

Off the wolf trotted, and went on and on until he came to the meadow where the first house stood, built of straw. He knocked at the door and the largest gosling answered, "Who is there knocking at my door?"

"Come, come," said the wolf, "open it, for it is I."

The gosling answered, "I will not open for you, because you will eat me."

"Open, open! I will not eat you, be not afraid."

But she still would not open her door.

"Very well," said the wolf, "if you will not open your door, I shall blow your house down." And indeed, he did blow and blow till he blew the house down. And then he swallowed the gosling.

"Now that I have eaten one," the wolf said, "I shall eat the others, too." Off he trotted until he came at last to the house of the second gosling. And everything happened as it had to the largest gosling. The wolf blew and blew until he blew down the house of hay, and in one swallow ate the middle-sized gosling.

Now the wolf ran on in search of the third gosling, the one who was the smallest. When he found her house, he knocked at her door. But she would not let him in. He tried and tried to blow her house down, but he could not! He climbed on the roof and tried to trample the house down, but again it was in vain.

"Very well!" he said to himself. "In one way or another I shall eat you!" He came down from the roof and, all gentleness, beseeched the little gosling, "Listen, smallest gosling. Do you not wish to make peace? I do not wish to quarrel with you who are so sweet and good. Tomorrow let us cook some macaroni. I will bring the butter and cheese and you shall furnish the flour."

"Very good," agreed the gosling. "Bring them then."

The wolf, well satisfied, saluted the gosling and went away.

The next day the little gosling got up early. She went out and bought the meal, then returned home and shut fast the door.

A little later the wolf came and knocked at her house, "Come, little gosling, open your door, for I have brought you butter and cheese!"

"Very well, give it to me here, on the balcony."

"Oh, no, indeed. You must open the door."

"I will open it when all is ready."

The wolf then had to give her the butter and cheese on the balcony, and he went away.

When he was away, the gosling prepared the macaroni, and put it on the fire to cook in a kettle full of water.

At two o'clock the wolf returned and called out, "Come, little gosling, open your door."

"No, I will not open my door, for when I am cooking I do not want anyone in the way. When the macaroni is ready, I will open the door and you may come in and eat it."

In a short while, the gosling called out to the

wolf, "Would you like to try a bit of macaroni to see whether it is well cooked?"

"Open the door! That is the better way."

"No, no; don't think you are coming in. Put your mouth to the hole in the balcony and I will pour the macaroni into it."

The wolf, all greedy as he was, put his mouth to the hole. The gosling was ready with the kettle of boiling water. She poured it instead of the macaroni through the hole into the wolf's mouth, till the wolf was scalded and killed.

Immediately then the smallest gosling took her knife and cut open the wolf's stomach. Out jumped her sisters, still alive, for the wolf had been so greedy that he had swallowed them whole.

The two larger ones begged their little sister's pardon for the unkind way in which they had treated her, and she, because she was kindhearted, forgave them. She took them into her house, and there they ate their macaroni and lived together safe and contented.

The Golden Lion

THERE WAS ONCE a rich merchant who had three sons. When they were grown up the eldest said to him, "Father, I wish to travel and see the world. I pray you will let me."

The father ordered a beautiful ship to be fitted out, and the young man sailed away in it. After some weeks the vessel cast anchor before a large town, and the merchant's son went on shore.

The first thing he saw was a large notice written on a board, stating that if any man could find the King's daughter within eight days he should have her as his wife, but that if he tried and failed, his head must be the forfeit.

"Well," thought the youth, as he read this proclamation, "that should not be a very difficult matter." So he asked an audience of the King, and told him that he wished to seek the Princess.

"Certainly," replied the King. "You have the whole palace to search in; but remember, if you fail, it will cost you your head."

So saying, he commanded the doors to be thrown open, and food and drink to be set before the young man, who, after he had eaten, began to look for the Princess. But though he searched every corner and chest and cupboard, he did not find her. After eight days he had to give up and have his head cut off.

All this time his father and brothers had heard no news of him and became anxious. At last the second son could bear it no longer, and said, "Dear Father, give me, I pray you, a large ship and some money, and let me go and seek my brother."

So another ship was fitted out. The young man then sailed away and was blown by the wind into the same harbor where his brother had landed.

Now when he saw the first ship lying at anchor, his heart beat high, and he said to himself, "My brother surely cannot be far off." And he ordered a boat to take him ashore.

As he jumped onto the pier his eye caught the notice about the Princess, and he said, "My brother has undertaken to find her and has certainly lost his head. I must try myself, and seek him as well as her. It cannot be such a very difficult matter." But he fared no better than his brother, and in eight days his head was cut off.

Now there was only the youngest son at home. Since the other two failed to return, he also begged for a ship that he might go in search of his lost brothers. When the vessel started, a high wind filled the sails and blew him straight to the harbor where the proclamation was posted.

"Oho," said he, as he read, "whoever can find the King's daughter shall have her as his wife. It is quite clear now what has befallen my brothers.

But, in spite of that, I think I must try my luck."

And he took the road to the castle. On the way he met an old woman, who stopped him and begged.

"Leave me in peace, old woman."

"Oh, do not send me away empty-handed," she begged. "You are such a handsome young man; surely you will not refuse an old woman a few pennies."

"I tell you, old woman, leave me alone."

"You are in some trouble?" she asked. "Tell me what it is and perhaps I can help you."

He told her how he had set his heart on finding the King's daughter.

"I can easily manage that for you, as long as you have enough gold."

"Oh, as to that, I have plenty."

"Well, you must take it to a goldsmith and have him make it into a golden lion, with eyes of crystal. Inside, it must have something that will enable it to play tunes. When it is ready, bring it to me."

The young man did as he was told. As soon as the lion was made, the old woman hid the youth in it and brought it to the King, who was so delighted that he wanted to buy it.

But she replied, "It does not belong to me, and my master will not part with it at any price."

"At any rate, leave it with me for a few days," said the King. "I should like to show it to my daughter."

"Yes, I can do that, but tomorrow I must have it back again." And she went away.

The King watched her till she was quite out of sight, so as to make sure that she was not spying upon him. Then he carried the golden lion into his room. He lifted some loose boards from the floor, above a staircase which went down to a door at the foot. This he unlocked and then entered a narrow passage closed by another door, which he also opened.

The young man, hidden in the golden lion, kept count of everything and marked that there were in all seven doors. After these had all been un-locked, the King entered an elegantly furnished hall where the Princess was amusing herself with eleven friends. All twelve girls were dressed the same and looked as like each other as twelve peas.

"What bad luck!" the youth said to himself. "Even if I managed to find my way here again, I don't see how I could ever tell which one was the Princess!"

He stared hard at the Princess as she clapped her hands with joy and ran up, crying, "Oh, do let us keep that splendid beast for tonight. It will make such a jolly plaything."

The King did not stay long. When he left, he handed over the lion to the girls, who played with it till they grew sleepy and knew it was time to go to bed. The Princess took the lion to her own room.

She was just beginning to doze when a voice quite close to her startled her.

"Oh lovely Princess, if you only knew what I have gone through to find you!"

The Princess jumped out of bed screaming, "The lion! The lion!" But her friends thought it was a nightmare and they did not trouble themselves to get up.

"Oh lovely Princess," continued the voice, "fear nothing! I am the son of a rich merchant and desire above all things to have you for my wife. In order to get to you, I hid myself in this golden lion."

"What use is that?" she asked. "For if you cannot pick me out from among my companions you will still lose your head."

"I look to you to help me," he replied. "I have done so much for you that you might do this one thing for me."

"Then listen to me. On the eighth day, I shall tie a white sash around my waist and by that you will know me."

The next morning the King came early to fetch

the lion, for the old woman was already at the palace asking for it. When she had the lion safe from view she let the young man out. At once he returned to the King and told him that he wished to find the Princess.

"Very good," said the King, who by this time was almost tired of repeating the same words, "but if you fail, your head will be the forfeit."

The youth remained in the castle, eating and looking at all the beautiful things around him and, every now and then, pretending to be searching busily in all the closets and corners. On the eighth day he entered the room where the King was sitting.

"Take up the floor here," he ordered.

The King gave a cry, but then stopped and asked, "Why do you want the floor taken up? There is nothing hidden."

Since all his courtiers were watching, he could not object further. He ordered the floor to be taken up as the young man desired. The youth then went straight down the staircase till he reached the door. There he turned and demanded the key. The King was forced to unlock this door, and the next, and the next, and the next, till all seven were open. They entered the hall where the twelve maidens stood in a row, so alike that none might tell them apart.

But, as the youth looked, one of them silently drew a white sash from her pocket and slipped it around her waist. At that the young man sprang to her side and cried, "This is the Princess and I claim her for my wife." The King had to own himself beaten and commanded that the wedding feast should be held.

After eight days the bridal pair said farewell to the King and set sail for the youth's own country, taking with them a shipload of treasures as the Princess's dowry. But they did not forget the old woman who had brought about all their happiness. Their gifts would make her comfortable to the end of her days.